What Is Grace?

Grandpa's explanation
to help parents
teach their children.

Special thanks and appreciation to Victoria Nordman for her editing, counsel, support, and loving encouragement.

Scripture quotations marked "KJV" are taken from the Holy Bible, King James Version (Public Domain).

Published by Michael Nordman

ISBN-13: 978-0-9998933-0-2

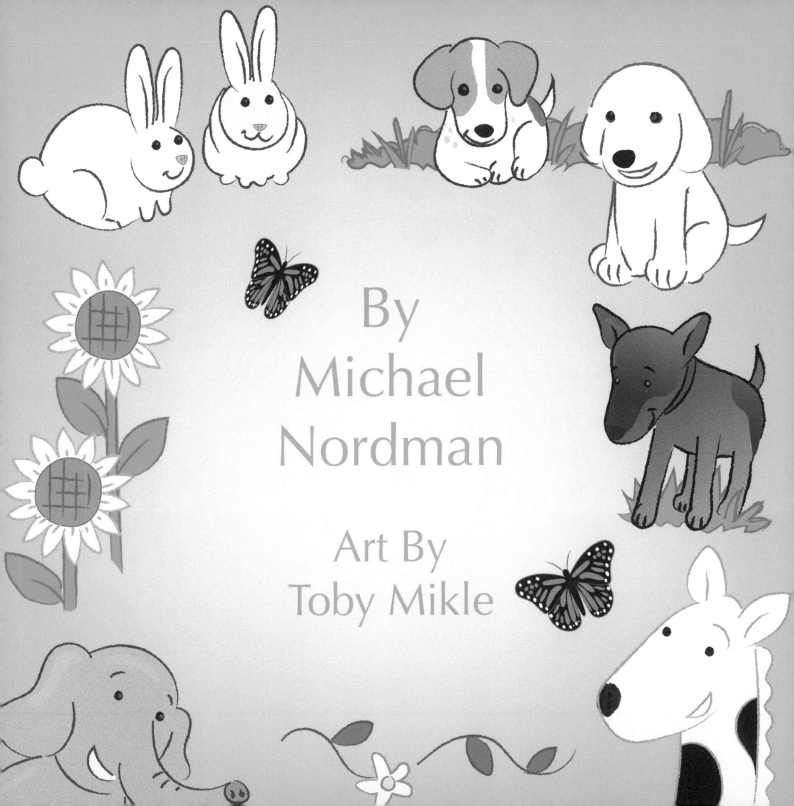

By
Michael
Nordman

Art By
Toby Mikle

COOL

DUCK

Sometimes words can have more than one meaning,

BANK

BARK

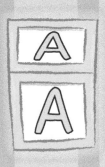

like the word
grace.

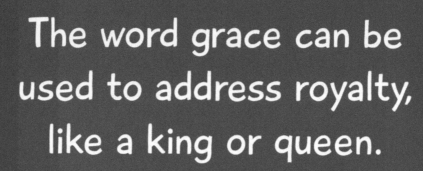

The word grace can be
used to address royalty,
like a king or queen.

7

"Yes, Your Grace."

Grace can be used to explain
an elegant style or act.

"She is a very grace—ful ballerina."

Grace can also be a prayer
that you say before you eat.

"Let's say grace."

Grace can be a little extra time
to return a book to the library.

"You have a five day grace period."

But, the most important meaning of the word grace is when we are talking about God's grace.

To: You
From: God

God's grace is a gift.

God saves you, blesses you with good things, and lets you into heaven because of what Jesus did for you.

When you get rewarded for something you did, like chores, you earned it and you deserve it.

You do not get God's grace because you deserve it or because you earned it by being good.

The way you get God's grace is by believing in Jesus and what he did for you on the cross, because he loved you so.

Jesus is God's gift
of grace to you.

To: You
From: God

For God so loved the world,

that he gave his only begotten Son,

that whosoever believeth in him

should not perish,

but have everlasting life.

John 3:16 KJV